ANITA LOBEL
SVEN'S BRIDGE

Greenwillow Books, New York

Pen-and-ink line drawings were combined with
watercolor paintings for the full-color art.
The text type is Cochin.

Copyright © 1965, 1992 by Anita Lobel
First published by Harper & Row, Publishers in 1965.
Revised edition published by Greenwillow Books in 1992.

Printed in Hong Kong by South China Printing Company (1988) Ltd.
First Edition
10 9 8 7 6 5 4 3 2 1

Library of Congress Cataloging-in-Publication Data
Lobel, Anita.
Sven's bridge / by Anita Lobel.
p.   cm.
"First published in 1965 by
Harper & Row, Publishers"—T.p. verso
Summary: Sven, a respected watchman on a
drawbridge, finds his work disrupted when
a thoughtless king blows the bridge up.
ISBN 0-688-11251-X (trade).
ISBN 0-688-11252-8 (lib.)
[1. Bridges—Fiction.
2. Kings, queens, rulers, etc.—Fiction.]
I. Title.   PZ7.L7794Sv   1992
[E]—dc20   91-29544   CIP   AC

For Susan
and for Ava,
with much love —
then and now

In a little village by a river lived a man named Sven.

Sven worked as a watchman on a drawbridge.
He liked his work. Every day he carefully
washed the bridge and oiled the machinery.

When boats sailed by,
he opened the bridge
to let them through.

The people of the village enjoyed
their bridge, and they loved Sven
for taking good care of it.

On summer days friends could visit each other
on both sides of the river.
"Good afternoon, Sven," said all the people.

In winter Sven would make a fire

and serve hot chocolate to everyone.

One day a big boat came sailing up the river.

"Look, Sven, look," shouted the children. "The king is coming! Open the bridge for the king!"

But before Sven could open the bridge even halfway,
the king cried angrily, "What a place to have a bridge!
So inconvenient when one travels!"

"Hurry, hurry," he raged, stamping his foot.
"I shall be late for dinner."

Suddenly the king lost his
temper altogether.

He shouted, "FIRE AWAY!"
The cannon boomed. . . .

And the bridge was blown

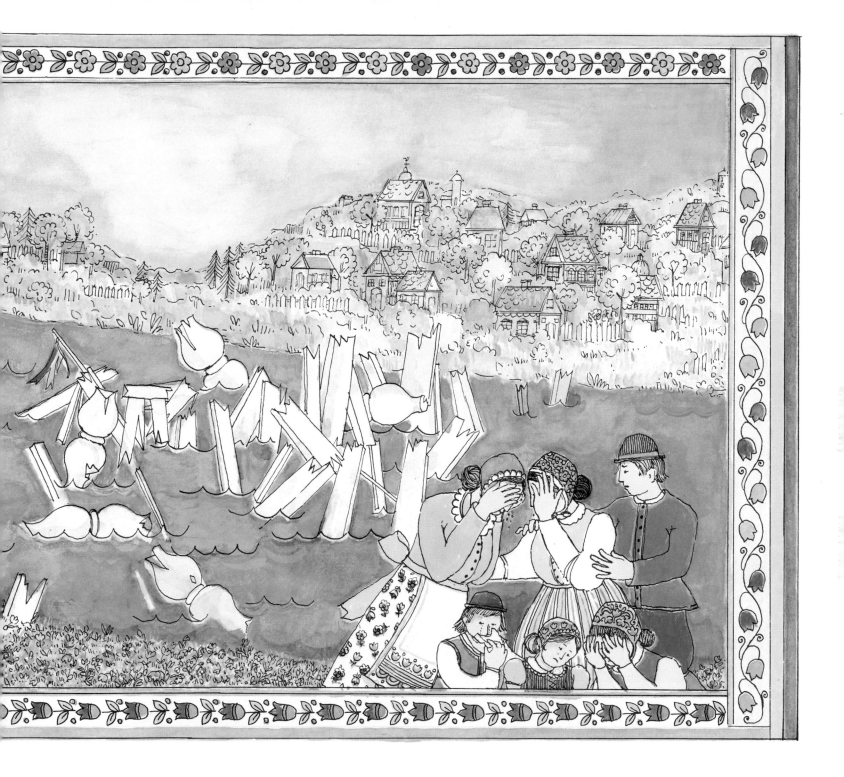

into a thousand pieces.

For many months the people tried to
visit friends, as they had before.
But it was not easy without the bridge.

Sven built a boat. All day long he worked hard ferrying people from one shore to the other. "It just is not the way it used to be when we had the bridge," everyone said.

Late one night Sven heard the sound
of horses' hoofs across the river.
The king was returning home from a party.

But the night was dark, and the coachman was tired.
And before anyone could cry, "Stop,"
the royal carriage tumbled into the river.

Sven rushed to rescue everyone.

As he helped the king into the boat, His Majesty
sputtered, "What a place not to have a bridge!
It makes traveling very dangerous!"

But inside the house the king recognized Sven and remembered why
there was no bridge. "This is all my fault," he said gloomily.
Then Sven served hot chocolate and cinnamon buns, and everyone
began to feel more cheerful. Suddenly the king had a royal idea.

"My bridge builders must come and build you a new bridge
at once," declared His Majesty.
"It would make traveling much easier again," Sven agreed.
And he served the king another cup of hot chocolate.

The very next day work on the new bridge began.
"This bridge will be very tall," the king explained.
"When I pass by in my boat, I shall sail right under it."

"That's nice," Sven said.
Perhaps the bridge will last longer
that way, he thought to himself.

When the new bridge was finished, all the people
from both sides of the river came to celebrate.

They threw flowers and waved good-bye to the king.
They kissed their friends and danced until dawn.

Sven loved taking care of the new bridge. He swept it and
polished it every day. And every evening, after the sun
had set, he hung bright lanterns on the bridge so that
travelers could find their way home in the dark.